Celeste Nites

Clarrissa Lee Moon

World Castle Publishing

http://www.worldcastlepublishing.com

Celeste Nites

World Castle Publishing
Pensacola, Florida

Copyright © by Clarrissa Lee Moon
ISBN-13: 9781937085094
ISBN-10: 1937085090

First Edition Createspace January 2011
Second Edition: World Castle Publishing April 2011
http://www.worldcastlepublishing.com

Cover Artist: Fantasia Frogs Design

Editor: Lea Ellen Borg

Printed in the United States

Clarrissa Lee Moon

Book One

Claiming Celeste

Chapter One

He watched her tonight like he'd watched her for the last dozen nights. She always came at the same time - at 8 pm and always wearing black. Tonight, she was wearing her black leather mini skirt with thigh high black leather boots. The black silk shirt she wore was cut into a vee to show off her nicely shaped breasts and short enough lengthwise to see her belly ring with a blue topaz stone hanging from the band. Her long auburn hair flowed freely tonight, framing her heart shaped face with wisps of delicate waves. She had the same routine of coming in, handing a twenty to the bouncer and then going to the bar for a drink. Not an alcoholic drink though, which was unusual for a woman coming into a bar night after night. No, she always ordered a virgin tequila sunrise. A fifty to the bouncer last week got him the story of why she handed the big burly biker the twenty as she walked in. It was to assure that she wouldn't be hassled by anyone at the bar or on the dance floor. She would hand him a ten for walking her out to the car when she was finished dancing.

He watched her as she sipped her drink while she stared at the dance floor. Most women coming in would be staring at the dance floor, sizing up who they would like to go home with, but that wasn't what she wanted. She wanted to move, to float and size up who she could get away with a little flash. She picked men…and women, who wouldn't mind a little tease, before she would move away silently to her own space on the floor to finish her dance. She was a most unusual woman. She came alone, danced, for the most part, alone and she went home…alone.

Same thing every night; night after night. It intrigued him enough to motivate him into finding out as much as he could about her, before he made his move to seduce the woman.

That was his first inclination. Another female to warm his bed for a few nights, then a pleasant parting and off hunting for a new woman to find pleasure with. Never staying with the same woman long enough to develop any emotional attachments on either side. He didn't have time for that in his life, but a man had his needs, regardless. And there were plenty of women who knew the score and went along with the game, night after night.

That is...until her saw her. Celeste, the enigma. The woman who has been dancing in his dreams for over a week now. And she was intruding in on his thoughts during business meetings, during the day, which burned him the most. As pleasant as women were, business was a time for quick thinking and making moves as one would play chess. It was NOT a time to be daydreaming about some pleasant fluff that would be gone by dawn and easily forgotten. But she had, over the last week, been infiltrating his concentration and he had had enough. He would seduce her, and then discard her, so he can get back to the business at hand.

He knew from watching her, she would be no easy target. He still hadn't figured out why she came to the bar to drink and dance alone. She was pleasant with prospective men who would come on to her, but she was also adamant about not teasing or giving in to their desires of taking her home. Just on the dance floor, would she tease and only slightly, never crossing that fine line between sensual dancing and flirting on the floor. So, he knew she wasn't here to be picked up or to pick anyone for the night's pleasures. On the surface, she seemed to just want to dance.

Her movements on the dance floor, however, gave away the slight tension in her moves of frustration and anger. He could see it in the sway of her hips and the tease of her stomach that she wanted something, but refused herself her own desires. Her face was strained with emotion, as if she was burying something deep inside and was using her dancing to let off a little steam in a safe manner. Control was her main strength. She showed her control in her dance, in not drinking anything alcoholic and in not leaving with a partner for the night. It was her strength, but it was also her weakness. A weakness he would play on to seduce her into his bed, so he could get her out of his system; to get her out of his dreams at night and during the day. She may not have any plans to choose anyone here to relieve her, after watching her for so long, but he had an idea of how to change her mind.

Like clockwork, she finished half of her drink and set it down. She took off her leather jacket and handed it to the bartender, whom she would have tipped heavily already to keep it safe for her while she danced. A song came on and she started to sway her hips while gliding towards the floor with the other dancers. She snapped her fingers to the beat of the music, her arms slowly rising up above her head, showing off her tight stomach with the glittering stone hanging in her belly ring, sparkling in the strobe lights. Her hips moved more aggressively as she approached the place where she wanted to dance, and people naturally moved out of her way. A few of the men, even though they had dance partners, beautiful ones too, would still stop and stare, watching her move. A few of the women, too, would watch, either to study her moves or to glare in jealousy for taking their dance partners attention off of them and onto her. Some would even look at her with a bit of desire themselves, which he found interesting. He knew this was the time he was waiting for, before she moved in between two other dance partners, where the woman did look at Celeste with a bit of desire in her eyes, and dance between them sensually, before she moved away again to dance alone. She always knew when to move the dance, before it became a tease or misconstrued as an offer. He slid onto the dance floor, coming up behind her and slowly molding his body to hers, matching her rhythm.

She tensed a bit, before he leaned down to whisper in her ear, "Relax, it's just a dance." He brought his hands slowly up her arms in a light caress, until their hands melded together. Feeling her allow the touch, he brought their arms down and wrapped her into his body and swayed with her while breathing lightly into her ear.

"I watch you dance every night." Smelling the soft jasmine fragrance of her hair, he breathed out, "I had to know how your body felt against mine." His body was hardening against her rear, as she undulated against him. He knew she felt him through their clothes, knew she felt his rising physical desire. Stepping back, he smoothly spun her around to face him, and then, before she could escape, he brought her back into his embrace and looked into her eyes. Sparkling blue, but with an eerie shade of green flame which sparked for an instant, as he rubbed himself sensuously into her body. He couldn't have seen green flame in her eyes, he thought to himself. It must have been a trick of the strobe lights. Shaking off the sensation, he floated with her, making sure she knew just how much he wanted her, desired her. When the song ended, he gently kissed her lips and walked away from her, leaving her alone on the dance floor without even saying good-bye.

He smiled tightly at his move. So unexpected. So damned clever. He will have her coming after *him* before the week was out. He was patient and cunning. He had to be, with his multi-million dollar corporations. He knew when to run hard with the ball and when to leave the ball for someone else to take to the goal line. He made his way back to the VIP lounge, to sit and watch her next move and to plan the next attack on her libido

Chapter Two

Celeste

Stunned, I stood there on the dance floor watching the handsome stranger move away from me. He was tall and slender, with an athletic build. His steps were strong, as he left the floor and he looked delicious, even moving away with a firm backside any woman would pant for. Tight fitting tailor-made pants graced him, along with the dark gray silk shirt he wore tonight. I hadn't been totally oblivious to his watching me every night. But, so long as he had stayed in his section of the bar, I didn't pay much attention to it.

Until now. He was well-built and handsome from afar, but up close, holding me so gently but firmly, he was devastating to my senses. Senses he didn't understand that were overloaded now from him being so near me. I could not only smell his expensive cologne that smelled of a heady mix of sandalwood and patchouli, but the sweet scent of his blood, as well, that had my incisors aching for a taste of his muscular neck, which was framed by his dark hair with the ends gently curling around the base. Longer then most businessmen wore their hair, but still stylishly done. His warm brown eyes burned deep with passion and desire, which almost had me asking him to bed me. I was already swollen and wet from him just holding me against him; which he'd done so I would feel how hard he had gotten while we danced. Feeling how large he was and how well he would fill me in both body and blood, I was tempted to take what he had teased me with. Whether he wanted it or not. Bloody wanker. Luckily for him, I was one of the few vampires who had a code of ethics. Also, lucky for him, I had more dire things on my mind then fulfilling either need of mine at the moment. Though, to feel his body in mine while I sank my teeth into his neck, sent a shiver of burning desire throughout my body and my pussy grew even wetter.

Damn him. The man played with fire, though he knew it not! I felt a warm hand tentatively touching mine, which shocked me out of my daze. A young man with hazel-blue eyes, looked at me with an innocent smile on his face.

"Would you like to dance with me? It seems your partner left you alone." He moved closer to me.

I backed away with a smile of my own, saying in a pure white-bread American accent, "No, thank you, but I appreciate the offer. It's time for me to be getting home. Maybe some other time?"

"Are you sure?" he asked. His smile was slowly fading away. He was smart enough to know there would be no 'some other time'.

"Yes, it's getting late. Goodbye." I turned resolutely to go back to the bar to pick up my jacket. Harold handed me my leather and I pulled it on, making sure the weapons I had inside of it would be quickly accessible if I had a need. It might have seemed redundant for a vampire to also carry weapons, but there were too many times my blades had saved me when my teeth weren't enough. I walked towards the door where Tommy stood waiting for me with an anxious look on his face.

"You didn't give me the signal when that guy rolled up on you like that. I didn't know if you needed me or not." He towered over me by two feet, making me feel like a small child in comparison.

I smiled at him reassuringly. "He just wanted one dance. He left right after, with no fuss. You saw. No need for you to wallop him."

His expression changed to one of relief. "OK, you just gotta make sure you signal me when you need help."

"I didn't need any help, as you saw, but I appreciate the worry. Let's go to my car so you can be back before your boss sees you walking me again." He had already been chewed out more than once for leaving his station to walk me. I would hate to cost him his job. I didn't really need him physically to protect me, but human men respected the sight of another male, more so than seeing a woman alone. It saved me so much hassle if I just had a man walk me out to deter any die hard wanker from the bar. Tommy liked the extra tip, and I had already tipped him heavily to NOT follow me when I gave that particular signal, no matter if it looked like I DID need help. But, that was for the other plan. Right now, I just needed to keep the men away who didn't take no for an answer very well. I was running out of places to hide the bodies. Those deaths, I didn't feel any remorse over; I figured I was saving some woman later on from being violated by removing the scum, but do it too often, and sooner or later, some smart copper starts putting the pieces together. So, it was better for me to avoid another episode, by having a big, strong man walk me to the car; though, inside I seethed over the necessity. Land of the free my arse, if a woman can't walk alone safely to her car.

Merde, I wouldn't have to do these ridiculous things at all if it wasn't for that foul creature hunting me. Oh, no,

I was thinking in French again, the land of my mortal birth, and that meant my anger was getting out of control. Normally even that would be all right, except that my vampire powers flared green in my eyes, when I felt any strong emotion. The British colloquialism came from spending a lot of time there, as the industrial era took over Great Britain. But, France was my home, in my heart and soul. I rarely ever went there anymore. It brought too much grief to me to see the changes that have taken over the land of my mundane birth. I knew that was the way of life; people changed, customs evolved, and the cities would reflect those changes, but it still hurt my heart. It seemed, however, when one has lived as long as I have, as you move from country to country, you take a piece of the land with you, usually with your speech patterns. Sayings and phrases have a way of sticking with a person, even though they may not have lived in that particular country for so long.

Here, in New York, they had so many different colorful phrases that I was sure would follow me for the next hundred years, if I could live through this latest challenge to my existence.

Men...they always start out so sweet, and then they turn into these awful, power hungry animals. I realized I had serious trust issues, but what woman wouldn't if she had a man trying to put a stake into her heart if she didn't do what he wanted her to do? What was worse, was the killing of the innocent men I had taken to my bed after leaving Henry. Yes, men could be vicious and heartless, but none of the ones I had slept with deserved what Henry had done to them. It was why I hadn't been intimate with anyone else for so long now. Getting blood was easy in New York, with its' underground Goth culture. Many dens had sprung up, celebrating the lifestyle of the vampire. My kin and I often frequent these places of people who wished they were vampires themselves and dressed as they thought a vampire did. Though true, I did often wear black to blend into the night, when I used to hunt freely. But no more - Henry killed those innocent people, as well. The underground dens were the only safe place for me to get the blood I needed. It was a bit sad for me to see so many lonely souls going to these places. People who didn't quite fit in with the current mainstream culture.

Truth of it was, these dens have existed for many hundreds of years. With some practicing black magic or having orgies, the venue changed from era to era, but in one form or another, these underground dens have always been around. They, too, have changed and evolved however, and it seemed that the latest motif of these places was the vampire. It made for easy hunting for my kind. And very hard for someone like Henry to find and kill my innocent donors. Getting into these places took knowing the right person for a long time, and when trust was earned, they gave you an address and the current password that changed weekly at most underground haunts. They had the ability of hiding in the darkness down to a fine art. The Inquisition and Papal hounds have made these dens very secretive over time. Just what I needed tonight, as I was now hungry after that strange but remarkable male who'd danced with me with such sensuality.

He would have made a fine lover for the evening, I sighed heavily. What a shame, I couldn't take him up on his offer, I mused to myself. I would hate to place his life in danger, so there never could be a pleasant interlude for us.

Chapter Three

Jacques blew off dinner with his brother, Armand, just so he could come down to the bar to see how his ploy was working.

Her timing was dead on and she went through her regular routine that finally had her on the dance floor. Again, he waited for the perfect time, before moving up behind her, since she hadn't moved towards his section of the bar.

"And how is my tiny dancer this evening?" He didn't wait for an answer, as he spun her into his body and allowed his desire to rise and tease her.

He leaned close to her ear, with a light breath, as he took in her scent and reveled in it. "I went to sleep last night thinking about tasting your honey on my tongue." He added to that imagery by lightly licking her ear, before spinning her out and back into his body with her buttocks pressing against his hard arousal.

By The Gods, this woman could make him hard so easily, he thought, as he felt her shudder against him. He could damn near smell her scent, as her arousal grew with his body practically making love to her on the dance floor.

It had infuriated him last night when a beautiful blond had come up to him after his teasing act with this tempestuous firecracker. She'd made the first move and he knew he could have taken her to a posh hotel and bedded her easily. However, thoughts of his tiny dancer had intruded, and he had declined what could have been a very nice way to end the evening. The blonde's offer made his body cold and it was easy to shut her down. This siren was going to pay for that, as well. He would take her until she begged for him to stop. No woman was going to unman him. All he needed was to have her for a night to get her out of his system. He knew it. He just needed her to come after him, just one time. He closed multi-million dollar deals all the time; he could close this need with her, too. He just needed her to want it more than he did.

She felt delicious in his arms and her body melted against his. She leaned her head back into him and he bent his head to kiss a long line along her sweet neck. She shivered and then tensed. Her movement stopped completely. Then, she turned to him with a look mixed with desire and need. Such a heady combination to his libido, and it took all of his self control not to bend her over in front of him and see if she was wearing any underwear beneath her tight black mini skirt. He hoped not, and his cock hardened even more at the thought of finding her bare and wet, ready for him to plunge himself deep inside her and fill her. With grim determination, he waited for the song to be almost over to lean his face near hers. "Anytime you want me, you know where I sit. Come to me and I will give you a night filled with pleasure." He gently kissed her neck again, then spun her away and walked back to the VIP lounge area.

The minx diverted from his well laid plan, by instead walking out the door with the bouncer for him to take her to her car. Damn the vixen. He smiled to himself. Well, there is always tomorrow night and the night after that. He wouldn't stop until he had taken his fill of her. And as before, he turned down offers for a night of relaxation and pleasant company. They just were not her. None of them. Once her had her, he knew though, he would be back to playing with the various color-haired females, who offered themselves with their hopeful eyes. But for now, no one would do, but that elusive minx. He would fuck her so well, she wouldn't be able to walk for a week without thinking of him. The perfect payback for being so hard to get. He leaned back into his chair as he fantasized about the many different ways he would take her, taste her and fill her.

No, she wouldn't soon forget him, once he had her. It was just getting her into his damn bed. Damn that vixen!

Celeste

Damn that man! Again, he had gotten me so damn hot and ready, I could feel the wetness start to trickle down my inner thighs. I groaned, as I sat down in my car seat, feeling how swollen my inner lips in my nether region were. Swollen with need and unfulfilled desire. But, somehow I knew that if I gave in to that damn man's seduction, he would wind up as the others had. I couldn't have that on my conscious. There should be no harm in just dancing with him though, right? If the man fucked as well as he danced...I groaned again. I had to get my mind off of having sex with him. It was just too dangerous. For the both of us.

Since feeding last night at one of the underground dens, I had no need of blood, but I would definitely need to go home and take care of my own needs and do my level best in not thinking of that damn male who'd that left me on the dance floor, throbbing with sexual heat. Often in the dens, sex could be had as well, but none of them made me feel that need, though the taking of blood could be very sexual. Often, I would allow my donor to stroke himself, as I fed from his neck. They got such a thrill from having their neck bitten into as they made themselves come. In the dens, a vampire can find whatever they needed and in any combination. It made things so much easier for feeding the way one wanted to. It was why the dens were frequented by so many different kinds of humans, as well as vampires. I drove home that night, cursing that infuriating male and conversely desiring him as well.

Jacques

Each night for the next three nights, he hunted her. He danced with her. He tempted her, but always she would walk away and out the door. Alone. He had never had a female resist him for so long. He tried whispering words of seduction into her ear. Telling her what he would love to do with her. As a last resort, tempted her with verbal scenes of love making, and still, she never came towards his table after he left her practically panting with desire on the dance floor. He knew she wanted him. He could feel it. He knew she liked men, from the way her body reacted to his. But, night after night, no matter the sweet and tempting words, or the slow movements he made with his body against hers, she would not come to him.

Tonight, he would try again, and ask her what it was that she needed to be enticed into his bedroom. He saw her walk through the door of the bar. He swelled with triumph, as he saw her bypass the bar completely and walk resolutely to his table. Finally, she was going to give in to him. About damn time - he was running out of ideas to tempt her with.

"We need to talk." She didn't look pleased. She didn't look like she wanted to dance on the floor or in the bed. She looked determined, but not in the way he'd been hoping for.

"We can talk about anything you desire, tiny dancer."

Her eyes closed at his pet name for her, but her face took on a dark look. "I can't dance with you anymore. So, please refrain from joining me on the dance floor ever again."

He was shocked. She was flatly turning him down and telling him to stay away. What in the hells was going on? She enjoyed the dancing as much as he did. He knew it from her movements against him. From the look of desire in her face as he turned her into him. From the way she shivered, when he would whisper some decadent position he would have her in, if they had been alone. And yet, here she was, telling him to permanently keep away now?

He narrowed his eyes at her. "Was it something I did?"

"No." She sadly shook her head, and that confused him even more. She looked like she really didn't want to stop, but was determined to end even this much love-play with him. "But, I just can't dance with you anymore. Thank you for the previous dances, but I'm asking nicely for you to stay away from me now on."

She looked around to the other ladies, who were sitting around, some not accompanied with anyone, but looking like they would like to be. "Besides, it looks like you can fill your time quite easily amongst this crowd. Goodbye." And with that, she turned from him and walked away without a backwards glance.

He couldn't fathom what the problem was. She looked like she was regretting having to tell him to keep away, but she didn't take back what she'd said. He was not the type to pursue a female who did not want him. No, meant no. Even if their body said yes, he still took it as a no and walked away. He didn't ever want to have a lady say it was a forced issue. He just sat there that night, watching her dance alone again, and get back into her previous routine. He respected her wishes, but he knew there was something else. Maybe there was someone else? But if that were true, why hadn't he shown up and spent time with his woman? Why would she come alone? Why did she look so damn frustrated and unloved, sexually? And it showed, in every move she took in her dance. He sat there confused, not quite sure where to proceed from here, but he wasn't done by a long shot. Not yet. He didn't run his financial empire of Dubois Enterprises by giving up so easily in a fight. He watched, and thought of every scenario that could be making her turn away from him, and some of the ideas were making him feel very protective of her. But, if she were in trouble, wouldn't she tell someone? She had that huge bouncer on her side, as well as the bartender. Surely, she had someone she could turn to in times of need? He'd let her cool off tonight, but tomorrow night, he was going to get some answers.

Chapter Four

As I walked out to my car that night, I was still feeling depressed. Dancing allowed me to vent some of the anger and frustration out of my system, but tonight, the dancing did not help. I got to my car and noticed another red envelope tucked under the windshield wiper.

I was shaking with anger, as I opened this new message from that psycho. Inside, in bold lettering, two simple words were written.

GOOD GIRL

Filled with rage, I crumbled this message as I did last nights, and threw it to the ground.

Last night, the message was:

STOP DANCING WITH HIM

I had no choice but to stop even that much pleasure with another being. I couldn't take a chance Henry would kill him, as he'd done to the others, if I didn't.

This isn't how the plan was supposed to go. The plan was to get Henry to come to me, so I can end this sick harassment of a mere mortal. Though, I hated doing it to sweet Henry, he left me with no other choice. I couldn't have him leaving the dead bodies of previous lover's trialing behind me or keep switching my resting place, so he couldn't find me while I was vulnerable.

He was deranged and dangerous now and not the sweet man I used to love long into the night. But the handsome stranger would be a casualty I just couldn't bear if this plan didn't work out. And, I couldn't change location, now that I knew Henry knew where I came to dance. The dancing was the lure I needed to draw Henry to me. Not to give him other victims to take his jealousy out on. I had been playing bait and rabbit for so long now, I was close to losing my mind, if I didn't find a way to put Henry down. I was tired of playing the scared victim, but hunting Henry had turned out to be harder than I would have thought for a human. He was very good at hiding, so getting to him before he got to anyone else proved to be a fatal mistake for too many people that I'd previously let get close to me.

I changed my resting place, my feeding dens and kept an unusual schedule in every aspect of my life, but for the dancing. That, I kept as routine as possible, to bring Henry out into the open.

I would have to go back again tomorrow night, but the handsome stranger had been a gentleman and had stayed away from me, as I asked. And from the sound of the message, Henry was pleased, too. The sick bastard. Ughh, I needed to get home and plan for the next move.

Jacques

She showed up again the next night. She went into her usual routine and glided for the dance floor. I got up and gave her every opportunity to motion me away, as I slowly approached her from where she could see me coming. Her face filled with regret again and I couldn't let it slide without finding out why she didn't want to dance with me anymore.

Moving just a mere foot away from her, I held out my hand to offer a dance and she slowly took it. Relief flooded through me, as I pulled her close and held her warm body next to mine.

"I thought of you again last night as I went home. I had been hoping you would be joining me?" I left the question hanging in the air. Again, offering her a night filled with pleasure.

She leaned back and her eyes were warm and friendly. She started to say something, but fear froze her in place. I turned to look to see what it was that had frightened her and I saw a man with a hate-filled face. He was over 6 feet in height and looked to be in good shape.

Dark brown hair, shaggy though from not having it cut and styled in so long; but you could tell he had been well-groomed at one time. At the moment, he didn't look like he belonged in such a club and I looked down at my tiny dancer and she spun out of my embrace, as if the fires of hell were following her.

***

Jacques saw the man go to chase her out the door and followed them both. The bouncer had gone to deal with another disturbance and didn't notice his tiny dancer was in trouble. He'd be damned if she would have to face that man alone though, and he put on speed to catch up.

He caught up to them in the parking lot, just as the man grabbed his tiny dancer, holding a wooden stake raised high in his other hand. It looked as if he were about to plunge it into her chest. "Turn me, or else, Celeste!" he screamed at her.

Jacques didn't wait for her answer, as he grabbed the madman and turned him around forcefully and punched him as hard as he could. The punch landed solidly,

35

knocking his tiny dancers' attacker out and he fell to the ground.

He looked up to see if she was all right and she looked pissed. "Damn it, you've ruined the plan." People were coming to see what the fight was about and she grabbed him, pulling him away. "Come on, we have to leave now."

"But, shouldn't we stay for the police?" he asked her.

"No, I can't afford that kind of involvement. Come on, please. We'll take your car."

He gave in, and guided her to where his car was and unlocked it before they'd even gotten close by pushing the button on his key-chain. They both climbed in and were off into traffic, before anyone could ask them any questions about the incident.

"OK, we're safe. Now, do you mind telling me what that was all about?" he grilled her.

"An ex-lover who can't get it through his head that it's over, is all."

"All right. Do you mind telling me why he had a wooden stake in his hand and was going to use it on you?" That one really baffled him.

"Henry is very deranged. He is homicidal and insane. Literally."

"So why not go to the police?"

"And what exactly are they going to do? Hmmm? A restraining order? You know as well as I, how effective that can be," she snorted. "No, I wouldn't waste my time."

"But, he was going to use a weapon on you. That could be an attempted murder charge."

"And how often do the jails let guys like him off on a technicality?"

"So, what was the plan you say I ruined?"

She slunk down into her seat and grumbled, "Never mind."

"You weren't seriously planning on taking him out before he did you?" He chuckled, "That is not a good plan, tiny dancer."

She just sat and fumed, so he changed his tactics. "So, is Celeste your name, tiny dancer?"

"Yes," came the mumbled reply.

"I am Jacques Dubois. We might as well go to my place and get you a drink. I'm sure your nerves would welcome it. Meanwhile, I'll call a driver to bring your car around."

"No, no driver. I can get my own car, thank you very much. In fact, why don't you just let me out here and I will find my own way home."

"You can't be serious. Let me take you to my home until things settle down back there and then we'll call for a taxi or something, if you still feel the need to flee from me," he grinned at her.

"I am not fleeing from you," she said defensively.

"If my tiny dancer says so."

He drove her to his place and walked her inside. Guiding her to the living room, he offered her a drink which she took, as she looked around at all of the antiques and paintings gracing the walls of his home. He very rarely brought a woman home for fucking. He usually took them to a very nice hotel room and then left when he was done with them. But, tonight, it just felt right to bring her home, where he could seduce her into his bed. For some odd reason, he wanted her scent on his pillows when he woke up the next morning. Tomorrow, they would figure a way to deal with this loon who was trying to harm his tiny dancer. For tonight, he finally had her here and he wanted a taste of her.

Watching her drink and seeing a small drop of alcohol on her lower lip, he bent in to kiss it off of her lips. She didn't pull back, as he licked the bead off her, so he moved in for a deeper taste of her lips and mouth. She moaned, as he kissed her deeply and he slowly moved his body closer, until they were as close as they had been on the dance floor. He moved his kisses to her neck and up to her ear begging her, "Let me take you now, tiny dancer. Let me dance inside your body. Please." He had never begged for a woman's charms before, but he did tonight.

Thankfully, she nodded her head in assent and he took the drink from her hand and set it down on the table next to them. He picked her up, taking her to his room, and placed her near the bed. "I have waited too long to be inside you," he simply said, as he turned her around and bent her over, lifting her mini skirt up over her tight, rounded ass. He moaned, as he realized his fondest fantasy of her had come true, as she had nothing on underneath the short skirt. He quickly took his cock out as he played with her pussy, getting her wetter than she'd already been. Gods, this woman felt wet and warm. He positioned his cock and slowly slid himself inside her. She was tight and hot, as he pushed in and out, slowly gaining more depth with every stroke. He needed to be in her NOW, and he pushed the rest of the way in to the hilt, burying himself in her moist heat. She moaned, as he moved within, and he played with her clit that was swelling with desire under his fingers. He could smell the musk of her arousal and hear her moan as he moved in and out of her, deeper and faster. This first time would be quick, but he needed to get this out of the way, so he could take his time with her later. He felt her nearing her first orgasm and he added more speed to his thrusts inside of her tight channel. She grew wetter for him and suddenly he felt her muscles constrict around his cock, making him groan as she came for him. "That's it, tiny dancer, come for me. Come for me, hard." He pushed into her deeper until he felt his own release near and he let it go, filling her up with his seed, pulsing hotly into her pussy which was still contracting around his dick, milking him dry.

He had never before ejaculated inside a woman without protection. But, he felt this deep need to fill her with his semen. He felt animalistic, as he came inside of her, spilling his seed inside her womb. He felt relief, at having finally spent himself into her, but if she thought it was over now, she had another thing coming.

He turned her back around and gently guided her onto the bed, while he lifted her shirt off her, baring her sweet breasts to his view. Just enough to fill a man's hands, and her nipples were hard and a lightly tanned-brown color. They looked so tasty, he had to take one into his mouth and gently suckle on it, while carefully massaging her other breast with his hand. He switched between her nipples, taking turns at each one, as she started to get aroused again under the onslaught of his mouth.

He pulled the skirt all the way off and removed his own shirt and pants. When he was as naked as she was, he put a hand on each knee ordering her, "Open for me, tiny dancer, I want to see you." She let him spread her legs wide and saw that her pussy was bare of any hair, and slick and moist from their lovemaking. He bent down to touch her gently between her legs, making sure she was wet and slick from pussy to anus, before sliding his finger inside her rosebud. He took his other finger and slid it inside her pussy while he latched onto her clit with his mouth. She moaned loudly with this new sensation, and he moved his fingers in and out of her, as he sucked and licked at her clit. He tasted her honey on his tongue and reveled in feeling her clit grow swollen from his suckling. The muscles of both her channels were tightening and he knew she was close to coming for him again. He picked up the pace his fingers were making, adding a bit more suction on her clit and she came apart for him with a loud scream of pleasure. She laid there shaking with her orgasm, trembling from the intensity.

He let his fingers slid out of her and chuckled with triumph, as he rose up to kiss her, letting her taste how well she'd come for him.

She started to push at his chest, prodding him to move away slightly from her. "My turn," was all she said. His cock leapt in response to her throaty growl and she pushed him onto his back, as she took his cock into her hands, which was already hard for her again. Her orgasm alone gotten him hard, but her demand for allowing her a turn got his dick pulsing in anticipation. She took his balls in her other hand and gently rolled them, as she teased the tip of his cock with her tongue. He shuddered, as she expertly played her mouth and hands on him. She took a finger and gently slid it inside of him, as she took his cock into her warm, wet mouth. He groaned at this double pleasure and arched into her mouth, waiting to feel her take him in as far as she could. She sucked at him gently, while she played with his ass and balls, moving up and down on his cock in a rhythm. Much more of this, and he would be coming into her mouth, but that's not where he wanted to spill himself. As he neared his release, he stopped her and moved her to her knees. "No, tiny dancer, you are going to feel me come inside you again this night, many times," getting behind her and filling her again with his large dick. Slowly, he started to move in her, building up the pressure between them. He leaned his head back, enjoying the sensation of pumping his cock into her tight pussy. When he went to look at her again, he saw from the corner of his eye, his brother, Armand, had come home and was watching them. Sexual heat spiked for him and he kept moving inside her. He guided her body up to his and she leaned back into him, as he played with her breast in one hand and rubbed her clit with the other, while dancing inside of her. She felt close to coming again, as he sped up his movements within and on her clit, and his brother watched it all.

Soon, with all the sensations he was giving her, she was crying out in another orgasm and he exploded deep inside of her. Something primal took over his soul and he felt as if he was claiming his mate for all time and it aroused him to know his brother watched him with this beautiful woman. His tiny dancer.

All throughout the night, he made love to her as he never had to any other woman. Over and over again, he would arouse her and then make her scream out his name. Finally, both were spent and he fell asleep holding her close to him, as he whispered to her, "My tiny dancer, forever. Je t'aime."

For once, his dreams were quiet and peaceful and the world felt right once more.

The next day, he woke up expecting to find her in his bed, sore from the last night's lovemaking. He smiled, as he thought of several oils he could use to ease her soreness and still have her moaning again in need once more.

She wasn't in the bed, however, and he couldn't hear her in the shower. He got up and then noticed a piece of paper on his dresser mirror on the far side of the wall.

His anger grew, as he took the note off of the mirror and read what she had written:

Jacques, last night was wonderful, but I can't stay. I have to make sure Henry doesn't find you. He is very dangerous and has killed previous lovers of mine. Please, don't ever go back to that bar again and he won't ever find you. I am going to lure him away to another place. Maybe, when I finish this, I can come back to you and dance with you through the night one more time.

Until that night, please be safe.

Mon amour, Celeste.

"She left you a Dear John letter?" Armand had walked in and saw him tightly gripping the letter in anger.

"She thinks to keep ME safe?" he growled.

"What are you talking about, brother?"

Jacques explained everything that had happened before he'd brought Celeste home, not only to seduce her, but to keep her safe until he could hire people to deal with this miscreant who would dare harm her.

"Man, you got it bad, don't you?"

"I have no idea what you're talking about." He said, dismissively.

"Good, then when we find her, can I have her next?" Armand asked, lightly.

That question both angered, and oddly excited him at the same time. To watch Armand moving inside Celeste, while he touched her, added a special kink to the love-play in his mind. He quickly let the thought go and got back to the fact that she thought to elude him again, when he obviously wasn't finished with her.

It was going to take many nights of lovemaking. Maybe many months. No, a year. Yes, a year he would give her. Damn it, the woman was driving him insane already.

"No, Armand, I am not done with my tiny dancer, yet. I may never be done with her."

Armand gripped his shoulder in sympathy. "You usually tire of them quickly and you have no problem giving them to us. Why is this one different?"

Often, he would date a woman one time and then tire of her. One of his brothers would then take her out for the night, but they, too, were like him. Bored very quickly.

"She just is. There is no explaining it."

"So, I won't have a chance to taste the sweetness I saw last night?"

"I didn't say that. I just said I can't give her up. Not yet."

Armand's eyes lit up. "Good. So, what's the plan now?"

"I go hunting for my tiny dancer."

"What about Francois in Europe? He's still trying to find out how Don Carlo outbid us on that land track in Southern France."

Francois was their youngest brother, who was in Europe looking after a deal there for Jacques and Armand.

"He'll be fine for now. There won't be anything we can do until he finds out how Don Carlo outbid us and then we will help him plug the leak. Until then, Celeste is in trouble and I have to find her before that madman does."

"Then, we go find her, brother."

Jacques snorted at him. Armand only wanted to find her, so he could taste her, himself. He needed to find her, because there was a strange ache in his heart that he had never felt before. Damn that minx; he could protect them both. Didn't she realize that?

No, she is going to have help in this problem of hers, whether she liked it or not.

Tiny Dancer, we will find you and bring you home, so we can keep you safe. And she'll be lucky if he didn't paddle that sweet ass of hers when he got her home.

He slammed out of his room. Let the hunt begin.

Book Two

Hunting Celeste

Chapter One

The way that man took me last night made me shiver every time I remembered it. My sensory memory would overload instantly, making me wet just thinking about how well he had danced inside my body throughout the night. He dominated me in bed, so sweetly and expertly, I wanted to moan in frustration at not being able to spend more time with him.

I could almost hear him whisper, "tiny dancer" in my head. I could almost feel him sliding his large cock inside me, filling me with his hardness and his heat.

Ah well, it had been a wonderful night, but there was no way I could stay for anymore delightful dancing, in the bed or out of it. I was sure by tonight, he would be back with his various red-heads, blondes and brunettes to choose from and most likely will have completely forgotten all about me and our night together. A man like him didn't stay with a woman too long. I knew this and could accept the reality that what we had last night was just a wonderful evening of pleasure. Though, if I were honest with myself, hearing him call me 'tiny dancer' and the gentle way he'd held me after his loving made me ache for something more than just one night with him. Especially with Jacques. Oh, and his name was even French. Merde. I was feeling like a school girl with her first crush and not thinking as a very old vampire who had lived long enough to have had escaped the French Revolution with my head still attached to my body. What was wrong with me?

No, I did the mortal a favor by leaving him. Henry would most likely think Jacques had taken me somewhere and dropped me off. So long as Henry didn't see us together again, he might let Jacques live and just come after me. I had left plenty of hints at the bar with Tommy, the bouncer, and the owner to pass the word to anyone who would come looking for me where to pick up my trail. I wanted Henry after me and not hunting Jacques out of a fit of jealousy. This time, the plan would work. I could tell last night, Henry had been taken in by my scared rabbit act and would make the same mistake all mortal men did in underestimating the strength of a vampire - even a female one was stronger than a normal human male. Now, I knew Henry had taken the bait and would try to bite again, if he can. I just needed him in a place where there were no witnesses and no one to come play the hero.

Damn that man! I'd almost had Henry right where I'd wanted him and he had to pull his Sir Galahad act. Though, watching him punch out Henry did give me a thrill. However, I needed to do this alone and not be thinking of a knight in shining armor who can make sweet love all night long to the point he wore out a female vampire.

Though, he knew it not. That was also a pretty heroic feat and my nether regions swelled again with the memory, my body agreeing with me. I growled in frustration.

No. I refuse to think about that damn man, who has already probably thought of his next conquest to hit on his list and has forgotten all about me already. I should know better. Merde!

Jacques

He and Armand had checked every bar and nightclub within a ten block radius of where he had first seen her. A week had gone past and he was getting frantic with worry. He'd even broken out his Tarot deck and had done a reading and got even more concerned. The first card was The High Priestess, but covering this card was the Devil. Two Major Arcana cards in first and second positions. This was not a good sign. It showed her being chained or shackled by her present circumstances. Below, was another card in the Celtic Layout that showed she had been chained down before, as well. This seemed to be a repeating thing with her life. What really worried him, were the amount of Major Arcana cards in her reading. Too many for her life to be mundane. He and his brothers rarely used their powers unless absolutely necessary. Only the amateurs and neo-pagans used magick on a daily basis. Though, he and his brothers were very powerful and natural born Mages; he only broke out with his powers during a crisis situation or for re-enforcing the protection shields around their home and offices. Others in high powered businesses weren't as scrupulous as he and his family has been with the use of magick for business purposes. Again, it's something he felt will, sooner or later, come back three fold on those who abuse their powers.

But this was different. His tiny dancer was in trouble and has left his protection in the mistaken assumption of protecting him! What a dear, but silly girl. Once he found her again, not only would he make sure she was kept safe, but he would teach her, one way or the other, how bad he considered she'd had been. He wasn't quite sure if he was ready for a serious relationship yet, but he knew he didn't want to lose her at this time. Deep down inside, he also could admit that he cared, perhaps too much, about the state of her well-being. He chuckled to himself; he would find her, get her safe, love her thoroughly until spent and then see where they were going with this. He bent down to pick up his spread and noticed the last card in the spread significating the outcome. The card was Death. He picked up his book and wrote down each card and their positions and then gathered them up. He wasn't ready to consider what that meant right now. If he had to, he would move heaven and Earth to change that particular outcome, if it was within his power. His tiny dancer was in grave peril at the moment and he needed to find her trail quickly. Maybe that bouncer might know something, although he hadn't considered it before, because he himself, would never tell a worker at a bar where he was going. He knew Celeste was very intelligent. Since she was on the run, surely she wouldn't have dropped any information to anyone there. He smacked his forehead with his own hand. Unless she wanted to lure someone to her and away from him. She wrote in the letter warning him to stay away from the bar from now on. She didn't stay with him because she was afraid that psycho would hurt him. Did she have no fear for herself?

How could he have been so blind?

"Armand!" he shouted.

His brother came running from his own room, asking, "What?"

"We need to go. I think I know where to start looking for her, but we have to hurry."

"Why?" He looked as worried as Jacques felt now.

"The reading I did doesn't look good for Celeste. I don't want to wait any longer."

"Then let's go."

They found out she'd left a good, clear trail to a bar in New Jersey. Thank the Gods, she wasn't too far away from them. He had ordered the jet ready and for a limousine to be waiting for them at the Jersey Airport. Then, they would get a hotel room and search for her until they found her.

On the plane, his thoughts of retribution on her sweet body were interrupted by his brother's quiet comment. "You care for her more than any of the others before, don't you?"

He grunted, "Maybe I do." That was all he was going to admit to at this time, even to his brother.

Armand sighed, as if disappointed.

"Why do you ask?"

"She looked sweet and very delectable."

Jacques thought about the past conquests they'd both had. Once either of them was finished with the woman, it was nothing to them to let the other have a turn with her, if she was willing. Most of the women didn't mind. Often, they would leave their doors open, even when taking their pleasure with a woman. Watching his brother have sex with a woman, even if he'd been with her before, had been stimulating. They never shared the woman at the same time, however. It had just never occurred to any of them. Passing on a woman when one got bored with her was normal for them. That is, until now, when his brother mentioned liking what he saw with his tiny dancer. Jacques could see Armand with Celeste, but for some reason, the thought of giving her over completely to him, he didn't like at all. However, he would like very much to see him with her, all the same. They have never done a ménage à trois with a woman before, but if it were Celeste, it was a very intriguing idea.

"First, we need to find her, then we'll figure out what to do with her."

Armand sounded intrigued. "Now, that sounds very interesting."

Celeste

I chose a seedy bar called the Down Lo' for two reasons. One, people who frequent these types of establishments didn't give a rats ass if some woman... or man...was getting killed in the parking lot. So, the odds of having some good Samaritan come running to the scene, or a bunch of gawkers to check out what's happening, was slim to none at the Down Lo'. The second reason, was there was a river not too far away where the body could be dumped. A nice secluded spot, but used often by those in the trade of dealing out death. No one would say anything if they saw me getting rid of a body there. I had everything set; Sir Galahad was out of my way. Though, I did think of him often, and how well he filled me that night. Ughh, stop that, I told myself. From the involuntary shudders that would rage through my body, it was obvious that it was going to take some time to get over having to leave him. I couldn't stay anyway, regardless. I was a vampire, and trusting another human with my secret was not happening ever again. Staying with them for any length of time, so they'd have a chance to notice something odd about me and go digging, like Henry did, was not a wise idea.

No.

Much better to just move on and forget how he tasted in my mouth as he fucked me with that warm look in his eyes.

Sacré bleu, I really must stop thinking about him. He probably has had dozens of women by now, and I didn't like to share, damn it.

Vampires were very territorial, especially once we've bitten a particular human's neck during sex. Though I'd refrained with every fiber of my being from biting Jacques, as he made love to me. The temptation had been almost overwhelming. Often, I wondered just how sweet and strong his blood would taste. Any more time with him in my bed, and the temptation would be impossible to resist, and then he would start putting the pieces together before too long. I couldn't chance that, either. There were too many cons and not enough pros in staying with that lovely man.

I sighed to myself. Besides, he wasn't the type to become a vampire's mate. He wasn't the type to become a human's mate, either. It was best to leave him behind, keeping him safe in the process and maybe, just maybe, keep my own heart safe, too.

When I went to the Down Lo', I went over again the plan of using some poor bloke in infuriating Henry into a mistake, like the one he'd made that night as I'd danced with Jacques. I hated using some poor sot for this, but if I could get Henry to chase me outside, as he'd done before, no one in this place would follow us. Then, Henry would find out just how strong even a female vampire can be.

Unlike the club in New York, however, these men with their lust, were harder to control. Most didn't understand the meaning of the word 'no'. It's why I had picked such an upscale club in New York, because the men tended to behave better, more often than not. Not so, at the Down Lo'. I've had to break many fingers as it is, and here it was, my fifth night in trying to get Henry enraged again into stupidity. Coming into the Down Lo' without a male escort seemed to wave a flag for the single men to come up and grab you, as if it was still the age of cavemen. I wouldn't be surprised if they soon carried clubs and started knocking out the smarter women to drag them off to their respective caves. Then again, a smart woman wouldn't come here in the first place, I would assume. And yet, here I was, alone and dancing with one of the overeager hopefuls in the bar. I kept my moves more modest then I had at the club in New York, so I wouldn't give off the wrong idea. Sometimes it worked and sometimes they got the wrong idea just from my very existence in being here. What were their mothers thinking as they raised them, I wondered. I had to grab his hand off of my breast for the fifth time and warned him with a pinch to his hand. I told him I would break his fingers if he couldn't control himself until the end of the dance. I never danced more than one time with any of the males here. That would have definitely been misconstrued as an offer for sex later. I sighed again. This was going to be a long fucking night.

Jacques

Jacques and his brother had gone to the hotel first to get settled in. Neither of them had any idea how long this would take, so they thought it would be best to have everything settled for their comfort and Celeste's, if they could manage to bring her along. That would be on the premise if they found her in the first place.

Armand was musing over the direct plan Jacques had come up with, which was to hit every bar on the south side, starting with the street name, Tommy the bouncer, had given them. "You know, since she bolted from you once before, if we did manage to find the right bar and she spotted you, she will most likely just bolt again."

"And what would you suggest? I'll have to go in these places and drag her out, if needed."

"Ah, the Neanderthal approach. I like it. It's a classic." He gave Jacques his most innocent look when Jacques turned to glare at him.

Jacques snorted at him, "All right, modern man. What would you do in my place?"

"Let my brother walk in and seduce her into going outside, then we grab her and take her to our lair here."

Jacques laughed, "Oh yes, that's much better than my plan."

He gave it some serious thought though. "Maybe you do have a point. If she sees me coming, she might not give me a chance to talk to her. It's not like we have a marriage going on, so me coming after her may seem a bit threatening." He was trying to see things from her point of view, so he could assure her of his intent, without scaring her away.

"So, you want me to search for her and bring her here?"

"Maybe that might be best, or at least to the limo. It would create a midway point in talking her into coming with us and helping her with her little stalker problem."

"Like we won't come off looking like stalkers ourselves, right?" his brother quipped. "I mean, you've only bedded the woman once."

"Actually, several times." He smiled ruefully, "Though, in a single night, true."

"Oh yes, I see how deep the relationship has grown then. Surely she won't take it as if we are stalking her at all." Armand said, drily.

Jacques just shook his head at his brother's jesting. He was used to his teasing and often threw it back at him when appropriate. His brother's comment of the word 'deep' though, brought back that night with the little minx. Yes, it would be nice to be deep within her right now. Other women still held no appeal for him. All he could think about was her scent, her taste and most of all her reading. It was worrying his mind and he couldn't help the protective feelings that welled up in him.

"Well, if you are going to let me take the lead on this, I ought to go shopping."

Jacques eyes widened at the statement. "What could you possibly need to go to a bar on the south side?"

"More common clothes. Armani might stand out there, don't you think?"

Armand

Armand had gotten a pair of faded blue jeans and a plain black t-shirt along with a battered leather jacket from a pawn store. That night, he started making his way through the many different types of bars that could have dancing inside along the long street. One after another, he crossed off his list, until he hit the Down Lo' bar half way through his hunt. There, he saw her dancing with some miscreant that looked like he was trying to latch on to her. He quickly went back outside to give his brother the good news and reentered the bar with the hope of taking her outside to the car to meet with Jacques. When he was back inside, he saw the same man trying very hard to talk her into another dance. He shook his head and waited to see what she would do. If she got into serious trouble, he wouldn't mind at all playing the hero for her. Gods, she was beautiful. He really couldn't fault any male for wanting to get next to her. He watched her deftly sidestep the man and proceed to the bar for a drink. He waited in making his way over, until she'd given her order to the bartender, before some other male took the seat next to her.

She looked up, startled for a second, then her face cleared in a cautious greeting.

He motioned to the chair next to her, asking, "May I?" Surprised at the courtesy, she nodded her head and waited for his next move with a slightly amused smile on her heart-shaped face. Her lips were glossy with a pink shade and looked so kissable to him.

"Would you like to have a drink with me?"

"I've already ordered mine, thank you," she said politely.

Inwardly cursing himself for the stupid question, he made another try. "Would you mind if I ordered my own drink and shared some pleasant conversation with you, then?"

"You have very nice manners for someone who frequents such an establishment."

"And you have a very nice vocabulary for a woman who would come to such a place."

"Touché."

"Is this where I should ask, 'What's a nice girl like you doing in a place like this'?"

"I think that's been overdone, don't you?"

His smiled widened, "It is a bit cliché, isn't it?" Nice side-step from answering him, he thought. She was smart and beautiful.

"A little," she grinned back.

He ordered his drink as hers arrived and turned back to her to watch her face.

He could stare at her forever. Her deep blue eyes seemed to be able to have the ability to flash with intelligent amusement to anger in a snap. He had already seen her eyes when they were filled with passion, though he'd thought at the time that they were green. Hmmm, maybe a trick of the light or something. Both colors suited her well, though. Remembering how she looked with Jacques thrusting himself inside her, made him hard from the memory.

"Would the lady care to dance with me, then?" he offered sweetly.

With a look of relief crossing her face, she replied, "It would be a pleasure."

He imagined it would be after having to put up with the rabble and their ham-handed ways here.

He let her set the pace and distance between them, moving slowly with her. The music played a typical bar tune, but the tempo was slow enough that they could dance to this song. The next song played and she allowed him another dance. This time the beat was such, that he could draw her nearer to his body. He groaned, at the feel of her next to him, but then she froze in his arms, and said, "You smell of him."

"Excuse me?"

She drew back and away from him. "You smell of Jacques. Is he here?" She frantically looked around, but didn't spot him and she wouldn't either, since he was still outside waiting with the limo.

"Now, wait a minute; please let me explain."

"Non. You even look like him. The scar on your left temple though and the clothes threw me off, but the scent cannot."

What an odd thing to say, Armand thought.

"You're right, I am sorry, but we need to talk with you, that's all. Please, let us explain. Let Jacques, himself, explain. He's worried for you."

"Worried for me?" she exclaimed, incredulous. "That damn man. Listen, I am not going to have either of you mess up my well laid plan...again. Both of you need to leave now, before that psycho I am trying to get to sees either of you."

Incredulous, Armand asked, "You can't seriously think to take a mad man on your own do you?"

"I can and I will, but the both of you will leave. Now. This isn't your business." She was furious and oddly, it turned him on.

"Fine, just talk to Jacques, all right? I don't want to see him hurt over this. Just give him a chance and listen to his plan which is much saner then yours. He misses you."

She stopped haranguing him for a moment and a sweet look crossed her face. Then she resolutely shook her head. "I miss him too, but I didn't ask for his help or yours. I don't need your help either, so leave now. I mean it or I will scream," she threatened.

His lips grew thin with anger at her stubborn attitude and he turned to walk away.

He went outside to the car and told Jacques she didn't want their help, which only seemed to infuriate his brother more.

Storming out of the limo, Jacques went to go inside the bar. Looks like plan A, caveman style after all, Armand thought, but he resolutely followed his brother in.

When they got inside, it seemed another man had taken his place with her on the dance floor. Jealousy shot through Armand and he had never known that feeling before in his life over a woman he hadn't even bedded yet.

Jacques was even more furious, as he saw that same man rub his grimy hands across her belly, playing with the belly ring with the blue stone she had there.

Jacques went to the dance floor, pulled the man off her and punched him so hard, he knocked the cretin out. Then, he grabbed Celeste's hand, as she started to berate him for it and dragged her out of the bar.

Armand hurried to open the limo door, so Jacques could hustle her into the car, ignoring her protest the entire time.

Jacques

He was so angry with her, he could spit nails. He didn't know if he would spank her or fuck her, once he got her into the limo. His brother was already there with the door opened and watched, with an amused look on his face, as he guided his tiny dancer into the back seat.

She started to say something but he hushed her up. "Not a word, Celeste." He was so angry at seeing that man's hands all over what was his. The thought made up his mind on what to do to her. "Come here, now." Moving her to her knees, he lifted her skirt and saw, as that first night with her, she was bare and wet already. His brother's sharp intake of breath, reminded him they were not alone. But, the fact that it was his brother, didn't take any of the heat away; instead, it added to the fire growing inside of him. He brought his hand down smartly on her bare buttocks and heard her gasp from the contact.

"How dare you," she hissed at him, but she didn't move away or try to avoid his ministrations.

His only answer was another smack to her ass and sliding a finger into her wet pussy, making her groan in defeat. He knew he had her, and now, he knew another one of her triggers. He wondered how many other delightful kinky switches he might find in his tiny dancer tonight.

"You've made me very angry, Celeste." Jacques growled.

"You don't have the right to do this to me. You don't own me." But the sharp retort was a small one, as he eased his finger in and out of her hot cunt. There was no conviction in her tone, but was actually one of submission and it made his shaft harder for her.

"I say I do." He unzipped his pants and took out his engorged cock, placing it at her moist opening. "And this says you are mine to do with as I will." He slid all the way into her with one long powerful stroke, which he emphasized with another smack to her ass. Her round ass was growing red with his admonishment. He rubbed the red mark and looked at his brother, who was gazing at the scene with desire hot in his eyes. He pulled out of her slowly, as he caressed her sweet derriere and then lay down another smack to her bottom. He followed though with another deep, hard stroke, punishing her for allowing someone not of his choosing to touch her sweet body. It didn't matter that it was on the dance floor. It didn't matter the man had touched nothing more than her bare stomach. It was the fact that another man he didn't know was touching someone he desired with his mind and body. If he was honest with himself, he also desired her with his whole soul. He knew he was being unreasonable, but this temptress made him feel out of his normal territory.

Knowing his brother also desired her didn't make him angry or jealous. Quite the opposite, in fact. He loved his brothers and he shared what he had with them, always. There was never any competition between them for anything, large or small. Thinking of his brother touching this vixen, as he made love to her, just made him harder. Thinking of someone who he didn't know or care about touching his woman made him feel insane with jealousy. With that thought, he brought his hand down again and pushed hard into her.

It made Armand groan with unconcealed lust and reminded her as well, that they had an audience. "Your brother..."

"I love," he finished for her. "So he stays and watches me punish you. It's part of your discipline, Celeste." He drove that fact into her, over and over again, making her cry with passion. He pulled out of her and made her lie on her back, spreading her legs before him. He took each leg and lifted them up onto his shoulders, so he could drive into her and Armand could still see her pussy being fucked.

Armand groaned again, and was unconsciously rubbing his own dick through his pants, as he watch Celeste being pushed into, over and over, again. The interior of the limo was filling with the scent of sex and mixing with her sweet smell of jasmine. A heady combination for the both of the men. Jacques decided his brother must see more of this beautiful woman as she groaned beneath his onslaught.

"Lift your shirt up, tiny dancer. Let us see your beautiful breasts. Come on, baby, show us, while I fuck you."

She capulated, as she lifted off her top and Armand moaned at the sight of her breasts bobbing, her nipples hard and pebbled, as Jacques pumped into her body.

She was moaning and looking at his brother, who was obviously hard, watching her being fucked on the leather seat. She moistened her lips at the sight and Jacques knew he could ask her of it now.

"Let him touch your breasts, sweetness. It makes me harder to think of him stroking and sucking your pretty tits."

She moaned her assent and Armand moved forward to touch her. He groaned as he saw his brother's hand close around her breast and begin to knead the soft flesh until his fingers rolled her hard nipples between his thumb and forefinger.

"That's good, my tiny dancer. Very good." His cock was swelling even more at the sight. "Now, let him suck on them, sweetheart. Let both of us make you feel good."

"Yes," came her soft reply, in between her moaning over the pleasure she was feeling now.

Armand bent his head and sucked a nipple into his mouth, and she groaned deeply from this. His brother was caressing one breast while sucking on the other and he could tell Armand was getting very hard for more of her.

She, too, was growing wetter and he could feel she was close to coming for them.

"It feels good doesn't it, tiny dancer?" He didn't wait for an answer, he was getting too hot. "Now, I want to see him stroke you clit while he sucks on your sweet breasts."

She whimpered, knowing he was bringing her passions to a fever pitch. Armand slowly traced his hand up to where her pussy was exposed, since Jacques had her lower half raised upwards with her legs hung over his shoulders so he could thrust deeply into her.

Her pussy tightened even harder around his dick, as Armand stroked her swelling love button. He, too, moaned with desire, feeling how wet she was because of their attentions to her body.

She caressed Armand's hair with one hand and grabbed the handle of the door behind her. She was moaning and gasping from the sensations they were overloading her with.

"Armand," getting his brothers attention, "taste her now. She is so close to coming. Suck on her clit and bring her off with my cock fucking her. I want to feel her shatter around my dick, as I pump my seed into her."

Armand moved up and licked at her clit, moaning over the taste of her honey. Jacques could see Armand's tongue flicking out and lapping at the bud as he pumped into her harder, knowing she was about to come apart.

He held off his own orgasm until he started to feel her shudder and shake. She gasped and then screamed in pleasure as she broke apart. That sent him over the edge and he exploded inside of her. Pulse after pulse of hot seed filled her contracting pussy, milking his dick for more cum.

Spent and exhilarated, he caressed her legs and eased her down onto the seat. Armand sat back and looked at her, his face naked with desire.

"You did well, Celeste, my tiny dancer, but we are not done with you yet, ma chérie." He eased her onto her knees again, though she felt a bit shaky still from their exercise so far. However, he knew from that first night, how to keep her going and wanting more.

"Armand, take my place."

They switched positions and he rubbed her ass again to steady her. "Shhh, lover; it would please me so much to see this." With that remark he slid his finger inside her ass and with his other hand, reached under to caress her now oversensitive clit. She shuddered in surrender and he nodded for Armand to take her now. Armand took out his hard and throbbing dick. Jacques was surprised Armand hadn't asked for relief with her in some form before now.

Armand didn't waste time and started to push himself into her now soaked pussy. Feeling how tight she still was and moist with heat, he moaned with pleasure, filling her up with his shaft.

"Gods, she is tight."

"And so very wet now, isn't she?"

Armand could only nod in agreement as he pushed himself in as far as he could and pulled out slow and easy.

He groaned at the sensation and filled her again with his manhood.

Jacques got a deep primitive feeling, knowing his brother was pushing his own semen deeper into his tiny dancer and would soon be filling her with his, as well. It was primal, it was ancient, this feeling; but he couldn't stop feeling it and reveling at the sight. It was making his dick grow large again, as he felt her muscles tightening around his finger and knowing his brother was feeling her contract on his cock. He rubbed her clit faster, bringing her need to a high level, before letting Armand take over, so he could get in front of her and offer his cock for sucking.

"Take it, sweetness. Suck me, while I watch Armand fuck your sweet pussy."

She obliged by sucking him into her mouth and flicking her tongue around the head of his shaft. Fire pulsed through his body and he started to fuck her mouth in rhythm to Armand's strokes inside of her body. He watched, as Armand pumped into her pussy with abandon. Jacques could tell his brother was thoroughly enjoying her. Armand's movements started to speed up and he knew his brother was about to cum inside of her. He slowed his own motion in her mouth, because the thought of Armand cumming inside of her, almost made him spill too soon. Armand let out a shout and buried his dick as far as she could take him. Jacques knew then, Armand's seed was filling her. He was hot and rigid with need again as he moved to take his brothers place, but not inside her pussy. His finger went to her ass, as he lubed it well with both of their juices. Once he could slide three fingers in her, he gently pressed his dick inside her anus, stretching her slowly and with care. She was tight and he was very wide, so he knew he'd have to be gentle at first, with his intrusion. She moaned deeply and Armand reached under her, rubbing her slit with his palm and making love to her pussy with his finger. She was getting very vocal about this, with her moaning getting louder and deeper. Once he had loosened her up, he moved more quickly inside of her and that made her cry out and beg for release.

"Please, Jacques, fuck me harder. Make me cum again."

He gave into her pleas and fucked her harder, as Armand quickened his pace with his hand. Just as he felt her clench down on his cock, she screamed out in passion and shuddered for them. His cock throbbing, he added his own shout as her ass convulsed around his dick, making him cum hard in her.

As they all recovered, panting from the excursion, Armand said with wonder, "That had to be the best sex I've ever had. She's like a drug - addictive."

"I won't be able to walk for a week," her voice was rough from screaming so much in pleasure.

Jacques grinned and smacked lightly on her ass. "Let that be a lesson to you then, my tiny dancer."

"A lesson for what? I don't have to stay with you if I don't want too."

"I swear, Celeste, if you don't stay, I may chain you to my damn wall. Do you understand?"

A look of pure fright overcame her face that he didn't understand. She liked being dominated and restraints usually come into the mix when having sex with that kind of kink. Why did the threat scare her so badly?

"Celeste?" he softly asked.

"Please, never chain me. Promise me!" She was shaking, but not in passion. It was sheer terror.

He gathered her up into his arms to comfort her. "Hush, love. Never, I promise. It's all right. Never anything you don't want to do. I swear it."

She started to calm down, believing his words. "Leather bindings I like, even handcuffs, if not left on for too long can add to my erotic needs; but never chains, Jacques. That would drive me insane. I can't go through that again. Not ever again, you hear me?"

"I swear. Never." He rocked her in his arms and Armand, too, feeling for her pain, came to cuddle her from the other side, offering his strength and warmth to her.

Once they both felt her relax, Armand went to the tiny sink in the limo and got a warm wet towel for her. He gently parted her legs to clean her and Jacques moved over to the other seat, contemplating what she had said, and more importantly, how she'd said it.

Armand guided her onto her back and spread her legs even more to get her clean everywhere. Her eyes slitted closed, obviously liking the attention and Armand leaned down to lick at her pussy.

Jacques picked up the phone, before they all got too vocal again and instructed the driver to take them to the hotel. From there, he would try to find a way to get her to stay within his protection and take care of her problem. Meanwhile, he would like very much to find out more of his tiny dancer's past. Why she had such fears and why she had such sexual desires. Somehow, he thought it might be related in some form.

Watching Armand tongue fuck her into another orgasm and then entering her again with his cock, Jacques was bemused at this strange turn of events. He cared for her a lot. He loved seeing his brother be with her. He could share her with him and not be jealous. Watching her get fucked by Armand was making his dick throb in need again, but he held off until they arrived at the hotel. Once inside, they both took her to the bed and proceeded to make love to her throughout the night and in every orifice she wanted to be loved in.

Sated and satisfied, they fell asleep together on the bed, tucking her tenderly between them.

In the morning, when he awoke, Armand was the one with the angry face and a letter in his hand.

"She did it again, brother."

He rubbed the sleep from his face. This was going to be a long fucking day.

"Let's go get her," was all he said to Armand.

Celeste Nites

Book Three

Sharing Celeste

Chapter One

eleste knew taking off, yet again, would really piss the two brothers off, but she had to get to a safe place to rest for the day. She was mostly vulnerable, only able to move in very slow steps during daylight hours. If she was caught in the sun or the curtains had been moved to allow the sun to shine in, she would slowly and painfully burn. There was nothing quite like being a vampire who couldn't hold her own in the sun yet. Oh sure, maybe in another two hundred years she may be able to withstand sunlight for a couple of hours, like her old Master could. But for now, she was still too young, by vampire standards; barely above a fledgling.

As she laid down on the bed to get ready for her daylight sleep, she remembered how sweetly Jacques and Armand had made love to her all through the night, until they had fallen asleep from exhaustion themselves, just a mere hour ago. Good thing too, because she needed time enough in the twilight to make it to her resting place in safety.

Oh, but could those men satisfy a lady. She was sore in places she'd forgotten she had. Jacques had surprised her with the requests of letting his brother touch her and make love to her. Armand was a wonderful lover and so oral about everything. He must have kissed, licked and sucked every inch of her body, from ear to toe. Yes, even her toes he took into his mouth and sensuously sucked on them. There was no place on her body he wouldn't put his mouth. Then, he followed with his dick, in any crevice his imagination led him. Jacques would watch for a while, getting aroused by the sounds Armand would elicit from her, and would soon join in with his own style of lovemaking. He was much more dominate and controlling, but gentle at the same time.

Not like her old Master, who was a sexual sadist, who had chained her and had at her any way he wanted it, whether she wanted it or not. And with whomever he'd wanted her to satisfy, or the punishments were severe when she would try to refuse. The fact that he was a Master Vampire and the one who had turned her, made him feel like he owned her, body and soul. She had lived through hell for the first hundred and fifty years of her vampire life. Those times with her old Master still gave her nightmares. Or would that be daymares, since she slept in the day? Whatever they were, it got bad from time to time, but she used to go looking for some pleasant distraction and would forget for a while. She would focus on just enjoying living again, free and clear. That was until one of her human ex-lovers had found out what she was and demanded that she turn him, so they could be together forever. When she had refused, he told her he would kill her and then himself, because if he couldn't have her, no one else could either, and he would end both of their lives.

Now, these two men wanted to spend some quality time with her. But, even if she could trust again, to share her secret and her love, she still had Henry to deal with or he would end their lives as well. She couldn't bear the thought of them coming to harm because she had been careless in a previous relationship. They already meant too much to her. Better they left mad at her for leaving them yet again, then to stay and try to protect her, only to wind up being killed themselves.

She turned in her bed and hugged the pillow to her body. A lone tear wound down the side of her face and into the pillowcase. How many times must she push people away? Even if not for Henry, she still couldn't let down her guard again. The risk was much too high. For everyone involved.

Jacques

Jacques and his brother made going to the bar for information first on their list, since Celeste had made such connections to the people at the bar in New York. They were hoping she had done the same here, but were very disappointed. The only thing that they did learn, which both of the brothers found amusing, was how many men she had broken fingers on for being overzealous with her body. This seemed to have the owner here actually mad at Celeste for it and blamed her for the trouble.

"I hope she don't come in no more. Bad for business," the owner told them.

Armand snorted, "Well, he has a very modern outlook on women now, doesn't he, brother?"

Jacques shook his head and looked around, frustrated with the results.

Seeing a man sitting at a table in the back, he asked him if he knew Celeste. No one inside the bar knew anything about her, since most of them were the daytime drinkers and didn't often come in at night.

They left, blinking at the bright sun, after being inside for so long with its dim lighting.

Probably to make even the most unappealing of customers look their best to one another, Jacques thought to himself.

He gazed up and down the street, trying to decide where to go from here, when he spotted a small gang of youths hanging out in front of a rundown market store at the corner. Kids knew things and neighborhood kids knew everything about their neighborhood. Jacques touched Armand's shoulder and nodded his head at the boys sitting in front of the store. Armand nodded back, silently agreeing with him and they headed towards the gangs direction.

The youths watched them with a cunning gleam in their eyes. There were five of them and they looked like they ruled the neighborhood. They also looked like they were sizing up Jacques and Armand, but these brothers were nobody's meat, in the office, or outside of it. One didn't make a multi-million dollar corporation prosper by not getting bloody every now and again with a pen or with a gun in some cases. That was a fact of life on any level of existence.

"Hello," Jacques greeted the youths, "I'm looking for some information."

"You're out of your territory, Mister Wall Street."

"Which is why I need the information."

"Why should we help you? You're not a cop."

"But I do have money."

"What says we just take the money and give you nothing, milkbone?"

"Because, we're not that easy." And with that, Armand showed the guns he had under his jacket. It looked like he had grown fond of wearing the leather and street clothes he'd bought to blend in. Jacques still looked like he shopped on 5th Avenue, which is why the boy thought his gang might have some easy pickings. Armand showed him otherwise and the boy grew sullen, saying, "Don't know shit, man."

Jacques pulled out a hundred and caressed it. "Not even of a pretty auburn-haired woman new in the neighborhood that comes to the Down Lo' every night to dance?"

A kid, a little younger than the one who had been taking the lead, hit him on the shoulders. "Tinkerbelle, man."

"Oooh, yeah, the hot mommy with the sweet belly button. Got to get me some of that one of these days hey, Ricky."

The boys laughed and Jacques face turned grim. "Where is she?"

"Hey, chill. Didn't know she was your twist, but it's gonna cost you more than that, Wall Street. Times are hard with inflation and economic stuff."

He pulled out two more bills to match the one in his hand. Inflation indeed.

"Chick's down on Silvertore Street." The boy held out his hand for the money.

Jacques held it back, asking, "Where on Silvertore Street?"

"That's extra," the kid grinned.

"There are other ways of getting information, as well." Armand again showed his piece.

The kid got a disgusted look on his face. "Man, chill. I got a kid to feed."

Sad thing was though, he only looked around seventeen, but he probably wasn't lying. The other sad fact was, even if Jacques gave him more money, the odds of the baby benefiting from it were slim to none.

"Not my problem. The woman is. Where. Is. She?" he ground out.

"2021 apartment 4c."

Jacques handed him the money and they headed toward Silvertore Street to get his tiny dancer back where she belonged. In his bed. Maybe he could tie her there with silk straps. His cock started to get hard at the thought and he grinned to himself, imagining her there with her arms and legs spread wide for him, tied to the bed.

Chapter Two

As they neared the apartments, Armand stopped him.

"Maybe you should let me handle this one."

Shocked, he looked at his brother. "Why?"

"Because you've got that face."

"Pardon me?"

"You've got that face on. The look of 'daddy is not happy and he is going to bring you to the carpet' face. You always do this when a member of the family steps out of line and causes grief. You pull that with her, now, and she'll just run again."

"But she did step out of line. She left us. Twice. She put herself into a dangerous situation once and she is about to do it again and I shouldn't be upset about that?"

"See? Proves my point."

"What does?"

"You're treating her like she is part of the family and in her mind, she isn't. She's made no promises. No commitments. She hasn't broken any of OUR rules."

That brought Jacques up short in his argument. Armand was right. What was he thinking? That's the problem; he couldn't think when it came to her - to his tiny dancer.

He caved in. "So, what do you suggest?"

"Let me go talk to her."

Jacques scoffed at him, "That worked so well last time."

"I know her better now. I think I know how to reach her. If you go in, you'll just wind up wanting to spank her and fuck her and we'll be right back where we started tomorrow."

Hearing Armand state exactly what he wanted to do to her, made his cock harden even more.

He pinched the bridge of his nose and sighed heavily, looking like he had a headache coming on. "So, what if your way doesn't work this time, either?"

"Then, we'll have to come up with something sneaky, but we can't force her, brother. We can't drag her home, tie her to the bed and make her a sex slave. That would be wrong."

"Tempting, though, isn't it?"

Armand grinned, "Very."

"All right, go in and try to reason with her. If that fails, we'll figure something else out." He wasn't used to coming up against a brick wall that he couldn't hammer down, one way or another. Celeste was proving to be very difficult to rein in. Damn minx.

Armand

The sun was about the go down, as he knocked on the door. He knocked again and she finally opened for him.

Exasperated, she asked, "What the hell are you doing here?"

"Can I come in and talk with you, please?" He gave her his best innocent stare. It didn't work on her, either.

"I told the both of you, you needed to get the hell away from me, before he finds out and kills you and your brother."

He snorted, "We're not that easy to kill, sweetness."

She growled, "Men."

He walked in, uninvited and closed the door.

"Is that a gun I smell?" she asked.

She could smell that? "This neighborhood is rough and I told you we weren't that easy to kill. I'll take it off and put it right there on the table if that makes you feel better?"

"Actually, it would."

He took off his jacket and hung it on the chair by the small dining room table. Then, he took off his holster that had his guns inside and put it on the table and moved away, to make her feel better. The place she was living in was a studio with no bedroom. Just a small dinette and one door that he assumed led to the bathroom. The bed was right behind her and there was no television. The place may have been small, but it was clean and neat. Almost austere. He saw two black bags and a suitcase he assumed she's been living out of.

There is no way they could allow this to continue, but he'd have to do some fast talking if they had any hope of tempting her to be with them.

There was a small loveseat and he moved there to give her more room.

"So, what's the problem with staying with us, baby?"

Her expression changed to one of frustration. "We spent the night together. I thought with guys like you, it would be a one night stand."

He shook his head, "You know it's more than that, sweetness."

"And it shouldn't be. I didn't say I would stay."

"No, but we want you to."

She started to pace within the small space in front of him. "I can't. It's impossible."

"Why, because of this loser who is stalking you?"

"Oh, don't talk to me about stalking."

He saw what she was trying to do. "Don't change the subject."

"Well, you both have and now look - here you are at my apartment without an invitation."

"We were worried about you. And yes, we want you to come back with us," he told her truthfully.

"And I said I cannot!"

"We can help you with this guy, honey. It's no problem for us."

"It's none of your concern." She was exasperated with him.

"It is now. You could get hurt. Anything can happen. We care too much to leave this alone."

She waved her finger at him, "I never asked either of you for any help in this matter."

All right, it was time to change tactics with her.

"Is it someone else?"

Confused from his sudden change in questions, she answered, "No."

"Do you like us?" he continued.

Grudgingly, she admitted, "Yes."

"Do you enjoy being with us?"

"Yes," she said softly.

"If this psycho wasn't around, would you be with us? Come stay with us?"

She said firmly, "No."

Ah, ha! So something else was keeping her away from them.

"Why?"

She tried to hedge, "That's complicated."

"I am sure I can keep up."

"I can't tell you."

"Well, it's not another man. Another woman?" He was confused now.

She laughed, "No."

"But you can't tell me?"

"No." She looked adamant.

This was getting him nowhere. An idea hit him. Sometimes, compromise was a good beginning.

"All right. What scenario would be acceptable to you that would allow us to be together?"

"None. Henry will kill the both of you if he knew we were together. I couldn't stand it if you two got hurt because of me."

Ah ha, again! "So you DO care about us?"

She rolled her eyes, "Of course, I do."

"Problem solved then. We'll find Henry, deal with him and then you will be in our bed." He added, "For a long, long time."

She growled again, "I still can't be with you. I can't stay with you."

"Fine, then we will just shadow you, keeping you safe until Henry shows up, and then we'll deal with him. Then, my lady, you are ours."

"You'd really shadow me?"

He looked into her blue eyes that were wide with shock. "Absolutely, yes. Even if you turn us away now, we couldn't leave you with that mad man after you. So, you're stuck with us until we know you're safe."

She almost shrieked and then got control of herself. "All right. How about this? Neither of you shadow me. I'll come to you both every night, but during the day I HAVE to be alone. As it is, I have to move again, because of you."

"Why? If we know you're safe and come to us during the night, we'll stay away."

"I can't explain it, but you can't know where I stay. Nobody can."

"Is there some other danger?"

"Only if you know where I live."

"But that doesn't make any sense." Unless she doesn't trust them, but why would she bed them then?

"It doesn't have to make sense. It's just the way it is."

Fine, baby steps then, he thought.

"So, that's the best we're going to get right now. You'll visit, but during the day, you will be in your new home?"

"That's the best I can offer right now."

Progress, then! He'll take it.

He had tried talking to her into more, but she wasn't budging, so he would try to seduce her. He had multi-million dollar deals that were easier to close then making deals with her.

She was fascinating.

"Then let's close this temporary compromise, baby."

He stood up and took off his shirt.

She had commented many times last night, how much she enjoyed his physique. He worked out regularly to keep his muscles tight and bulging just right. Her hands had been everywhere on him, touching his corded strength. Her hot mouth had followed as well, and she had such a talented little tongue. His cock grew hard, thinking about her sweet mouth on him again and he moved slowly towards her.

"That first night when you were with Jacques, I watched you. I was passing his bedroom on the way to mine and saw him behind you, fucking you. The sight of your body, as he pushed himself inside you, got me so hard, like I am now."

Her face looked like she'd been caught in a trap like a rabbit. She stood immobile as he moved closer, afraid to startle her. He unzipped his pants and took out his dick and began to stroke it for her.

"Watching him fuck you was the most erotic thing I have ever seen. I have seen him with other women and it got me excited," he confessed. "But you were amazing. Jacques made sure I could see how he held your breast with one hand, while he stroked your clit with the other. I saw how wet and how fucking hot you were for him." He kept the strokes on his cock slow and steady, watching her lick her lips, as if she could almost taste him.

"I went to my room that first time and masturbated, thinking of your hot pussy on my shaft." He shucked off his boots one by one. His hand moved up and down his hard length, teasing her with the sight of him.

"Take your shirt off, baby. Let me see your breasts again, like that night. Like last night."

Her breath was coming faster, as she took off her top for him.

"That's good, baby. They're so beautiful." He took off his pants and was standing there naked and hard for her, and still, he stroked his cock.

"A bit later, I heard you cry out so loudly, I had to go see what Jacques was doing with you. What I saw, had me fucking hard all over again. He had your legs spread and was licking your pussy. Do you remember?"

She nodded her head slowly, her breath coming faster from desire of him and what he was making her recall.

"When Jacques felt me there, he spread your legs wider for me, so I could see him licking you. He sucked at your clit, then lapped up the cream he made. Over and over, he slid his tongue down to your ass and laved you 'till you moaned again." He stroked his dick a bit faster for her. "Remember what he did next?"

Again, she could only nod. He could see her nipples were hard and needing attention.

"Touch your nipples for me. Play with them."

She reached up with her hands and started to knead her breasts. Slowly, she moved in and played with her nipples until he saw her mouth part slightly. He could tell she was getting hotter, but he just teased her some more. "I remembered what he did, too. He speared your hot cunt with his tongue and fucked you with it. It made me so fucking hot. I started to stroke my dick right there, under my robe, as I watched him lap up your juices. You cried out and squirmed, but he didn't let up. He just kept licking your sweet pussy and made sure I saw everything. How wet you were. How pink your pussy was and how sweetly you moaned when he would get you close to an orgasm. He finally made you come, and I came again, watching how soaked you'd gotten. How you were practically fucking his tongue, his face. I wanted to taste your pussy so bad, I almost went in and asked. But, I just stood there watching you come with him licking all your honey off. Honey I wanted for myself. Take your skirt off, sweetness. I want to see that pretty pink pussy of yours again. I want to see if it's getting wet for me."

She removed the skirt and he saw she was bare, as usual, and wonderfully wet.

"Get on the bed and lie back, baby."

The bed was behind her and she lie on it. He got on the bed in front of her. "Come on, baby. Spread your legs for me. Let me see it all."

She did what he asked and he moved in between her legs, still on his knees and stroking his cock faster, seeing how wet she had gotten.

"That's good, baby. Now, play with your pussy. Slide a finger in and fuck yourself for me." He watched her touch her cunt and slowly slide a finger inside herself, moving it in and out. He kept moving his hand up and down his shaft from the head to the base, up and down, while he watched her pleasure herself, as well.

"I'd gone back to my room, thinking he'd be done with you soon. I was thinking and hoping you would be a one night stand, so I could have you next. I knew things were different, when he kept taking you over and over again. I'd hear you cry out, and then I would hear him

111

come. So many times, you pleasured each other that night. I couldn't sleep, but I didn't care. I just wanted so much to be the one in you next. Hours later, you two were still at it. I got up and went to see what was going on. You were on your knees before him, sucking his dick into that hot mouth of yours. Your ass was up in the air and I could see how well he had been fucking you. You were wet and swollen. I could see everything, while you sucked him off. When he saw me watching again, he started to fuck your mouth, making your ass move around a bit. I was so tempted to come up behind you and stick my dick in you, while you licked his cock. We'd never shared a woman at the same time before, but seeing you suckle him and that sweet round ass of yours, I wondered what it would be like with you. Last night, I got to find out how it would be to be inside that tight pussy of yours, while you sucked Jacques' dick. Knowing he was coming in your hot mouth while I fucked you, was the hottest thing I have ever felt." He sped up the motion on his cock, moving his hand faster, as he neared his release. He moved down, so his cock would almost be touching her pussy she'd been fucking with her finger.

"Celeste, baby, I am going to come," he moaned, as he came on her pussy. He let himself finish inside her, after he removed her hand and slid his dick into her. He gathered her in his arms while he shuddered the rest of his release.

"Baby, I love being with you." He kissed the side of her neck. "I love watching Jacques make love to you."

He slid his now spent cock out of her and moved down between her legs. "But, most of all, I love tasting your pussy."

He spread her legs wide and began lapping up her juices. Then, he started sucking on her clit, which had her screaming her own release into his mouth. He sucked down her nectar and kept licking her labia, her inner folds and then up to her clitoris and sucked it gently back into his mouth. He'd roll his tongue around and suckle the nub at the same time and brought her to climax again. By that time, his cock was hard and ready for her, once more. He slid up her body and kissed her, as he pushed inside of her.

"It's not just the sex," he whispered, while moving in and out of her channel. "You're so smart and independent, beautiful and funny." His movements were harder and moved deeper inside her now. "But, I really can't think when I'm fucking you, baby." He started to pound into her deeper. She was crying out loudly, taking everything he gave her.

"I just really need to - fuck - you - right - now!"

She grabbed onto him and held on, while he started to thrust into her so hard, the bed was banging into the wall behind them. Still, he didn't stop and kept building the speed, until he saw stars burst behind his eyelids, as he ejaculated into her. He felt her muscles contract around his dick, as well, letting him know she had made the trip with him.

Panting hard, he looked at her, worried he might have taken it too far. "Are you all right, baby?'

Grinning and trying to regain her own breath, she whispered, "Oh, yeah."

They laughed together and then heard a throat clear in the room with them.

They both looked up to see Jacques standing in the room near the door.

"I came to see what was taking so long and then heard the pounding on the walls." He actually looked embarrassed. "I thought someone might be having a problem and the door was unlocked, but I guess things are all right."

"No worries, brother. We're just compromising," Armand grinned up at his brother.

"Oh, is that what this is? I have to ask though, is there any left for me?"

Celeste groaned out, "Give me fifteen minutes and then we'll talk about it."

Jacques started taking off his shirt. "I've got a better idea. Just spread your legs and I'll kiss it all better, tiny dancer."

Celeste Nites

THE END

Please come and read Celeste Nites second trilogy:

Protecting Celeste, Contemplating Celeste and Loving Celeste ^{TBA}

Also, for your reading pleasure: A paranormal action series:

Memoirs of the Nightwolves Series

Nightwolves Coalition...available now

Nightwolves on the Prowl...available now

Nightwolves Sirens Song...available now

Nightwolves Dawn to Dusk (Semi Prequel)...(TBA)

Nightwolves Battle for Kla' din...(TBA)

Nightwolves Union on Trinidad...(TBA)

Nightwolves Twilight - The Last Battle...(TBA)

Nightwolves Companion - What was Real, Mundane and Magick...(TBA)

Connect with me at the Nightwolves Lair Blog -
http://clarrissamoon.blogspot.com/
http://www.clarrissaleemoonauthor.com

Author Bio

Clarrissa Moon would like to live like a tumbleweed, going from different states often, but her home base is in Tucson, Arizona. She's an avid reader and owner of more books and DVD's then any used book shop; she also enjoys Martial arts, swimming and raising pure bred Japanese Chins. She has written as a journalist for two E-magazines. She is also, the author of 'Celeste's Nites' Novelettes. She considers herself unique, unusual and unconquerable

In Honor of our Planet's wild animals:
Please help these Organizations that save our Endangered Species such as the Wolves and Silverback gorillas.
http://www.defenders.org/
http://www.bigoakwolfsanctuary.org/
http://gorillafund.org/

Celtic Circle + Pyramid

J&T&T

Clarrissa Lee Moon

Find C

Celeste Nites